More Fables of Aesop

MORE
fables of
ÆSOP

Retold and illustrated
by JACK KENT

Parents' Magazine Press · New York

Library of Congress Cataloging in Publication Data

Kent, Jack, 1920—
    More fables of Aesop.
    SUMMARY: New versions of fourteen more old fables.
    1. Fables. [1. Fables] I. Aesopus. Fabulae.
II. Title.
PZ8.2.K45Mo   398.2'452 [E]   73-13635
ISBN 0-8193-0750-5   ISBN 0-8193-0751-3 (lib. bdg.)

CONTENTS

The fables of Aesop have appeared in many forms since they were first collected and set down by him some twenty-five hundred years ago. Socrates himself made poems of some of them, and writers have been embellishing them ever since. By means of his artwork, Jack Kent has developed a fresh variation. Freely using the V. S. Vernon-Jones version as a point of departure, he has given the stories a new dimension of humor and, while the morals are as true as ever, the reader enjoys a chuckle along with the verities.

THE WOLF
AND THE LION

A wolf, having stolen a lamb from
a fold, was carrying it off to his lair.

On the way he met a lion who seized
the lamb and took it from him.

Standing at a safe distance, the
wolf exclaimed, "You thief! That
lamb belongs to me!"

To which the lion jeeringly replied,
"Belongs to you, does it? It was
given to you by a friend, I suppose."

*One who steals has no right to complain
if he's robbed.*

THE MAN AND THE SATYR

A man and a satyr were traveling together.

One cold day the man blew on his hands.
"Why did you do that?" asked the satyr.

"I blew on my hands to warm them,"
the man explained.

They stopped at an inn for supper.
The man blew on the hot soup.

"Why did you do that?" asked the satyr.
"I blew on my soup to cool it," the
man explained.

The satyr ran away, saying, "I want nothing to do with anyone who can blow hot and cold with the same breath!"

We don't trust what we don't understand.

THE HARE AND THE TORTOISE

The hare teased the tortoise about being so pokey.
"I get where I'm going as surely as YOU do!"
said the tortoise.

"But I get where I'm going
FASTER," said the hare.

The fox suggested they run a race to settle
the argument.

The hare laughed so hard at the idea
that it made the tortoise angry. "I'll
race you and I'll WIN!" the tortoise said.

The race had hardly begun before the
speedy hare was out of sight.

The hare was so sure of himself
that he lay down by the side of the
path to take a short nap.

The tortoise kept plodding slowly along.

The hare woke up just in time
to see the tortoise cross the
finish line and win the race.

FINISH

Slow and steady wins the race.

THE HARE AND
THE HOUND

A hound startled a hare,
but after a long run,
gave up the chase.

A goatherd mocked him, saying,
"The little one is the better runner."

The hound replied, "You do not see the difference
between us: I was only running for a dinner,
but he was running for his life."

*WHY we do a thing often determines HOW
we do it.*

THE FOX AND THE CRANE

A fox invited a crane to supper
and served nothing but some soup
in a broad flat dish.

The crane, with his long bill, was
unable to eat anything.
The fox thought it was a good joke.

The crane, in his turn, asked the fox to sup with him. The food was served in a flagon with a long narrow mouth. The fox couldn't even get a taste of it.

Sometimes a dose of our own medicine is good for us.

THE CROW AND THE PITCHER

A thirsty crow found
a pitcher with a little
water in the bottom.
But he couldn't reach it.

He collected
a number of
pebbles.

Then he dropped
them one by one
into the pitcher.
Each pebble
raised the water
a little higher.

And at last
the crow could
reach it and
get a drink.

Little by little does the job.

THE BOY AND
THE FILBERTS

A boy reached into
a jar of filberts
and grabbed as many
as he could.

But then he couldn't
pull his hand out
again. The neck of
the jar was too small
for such a big fistful.

The boy pulled and pulled, but got nowhere. He sat down and cried.

A passerby saw the boy's problem and said to him, "Be satisfied with half the amount and you'll have no trouble getting your hand out."

Don't be greedy.

THE GRASSHOPPER
AND THE ANTS

All summer long the grasshopper
sat in the sunshine and sang.

While the ants were busily
gathering food for the winter.

Winter came and
the hungry grasshopper
asked the ants for
a bite to eat.

But the ants sent him away, saying, "If you were foolish enough to sing all the summer, you must dance supperless to bed in the winter."

You can't play all the time.

THE LION AND THE MOUSE

A mouse woke a sleeping lion. The angry lion was about to kill him when the mouse said, "Please don't hurt me and someday I'll do YOU a favor." "What can a mouse do for a lion?" the lion asked. But he let the mouse go.

Shortly after this, the
lion was caught in a
hunter's snare.

When the mouse saw the trouble the lion was in,
he gnawed through the rope and set him free.

"You laughed at the idea of my
ever being of use to you," said
the mouse. "But now you see that
it is possible for even a mouse
to help a lion."

*All of us, the great
and the little,
have need of each other.*

35

THE CAT AND VENUS

A cat was in love with a
handsome young man.

She asked Venus, the
goddess of love, to turn
her into a woman.

And Venus did.

The young man fell in
love with her and they
were married.

A short while later the young bride
saw a mouse.

Forgetting that she wasn't a cat
anymore, she chased the mouse.

Venus was so disgusted with her
that she turned her back into a cat.

*It's easier to change our looks
than it is to change our habits.*

THE BEAR AND THE TWO TRAVELERS

Two travelers came face
to face with a hungry bear.

One man quickly
climbed a tree.
The other, having
nowhere to hide,
lay down and
played dead.

Bears don't eat
dead things, so
the bear
went away.

The man in the tree climbed down and
jokingly said, "I noticed the bear put
his mouth close to your ear. What
did he whisper to you?"

"He gave me this advice," his companion
replied, "never travel with a friend who
deserts you at the first sign of danger."

Misfortune tests the sincerity of friends.

THE NORTH WIND AND THE SUN

The North Wind and the Sun argued
as to which was the stronger.

They agreed that the winner should be
the one who could first strip a wayfaring
man of his clothes.

The North Wind tried first. He blew
with all his might. But the keener his blasts,
the closer the traveler wrapped his cloak
around him.

At last the Wind gave up and called upon the Sun
to see what he could do.

The Sun shone out with all his warmth.
The traveler soon took off one
garment after another.

Finally he removed all his clothes and took
a sun bath.

Persuasion is better than force.

BELLING THE CAT

The mice held a meeting to decide what to do
to protect themselves from the cat.
One mouse suggested that they tie a bell around
his neck so they could hear him coming.

"Belling the cat is
a good idea," one old
mouse said...

"But which of us is going to do it?"

Some things are easier said than done.

53

THE FLY ON THE WAGON

A farm wagon rumbled down a dirt road, stirring up clouds of dust.

A fly that was sitting in the back of the wagon said, "My, my! we're raising a lot of dust, aren't we?"

We sometimes take credit for more than we do.

JACK KENT is the author-illustrator of *The Wizard of Wallaby Wallow, The Fat Cat, Mr. Meebles, The Blah, The Grown-up Day* and *Just Only John* as well as *Jack Kent's Fables of Aesop* and *Jack Kent's Twelve Days of Christmas*, all published by Parents' Magazine Press. Mr. Kent is a free-lance commercial artist and the creator of the comic strip, *King Aroo*. He was born in Burlington, Iowa, and because his family traveled constantly, he received his education at "public and private schools in a long list of cities and states." He was living in San Antonio, Texas, when a local newspaper sent a reporter to interview him in connection with *King Aroo*. He married the reporter and they are still living in San Antonio, with their son, Jack Jr.